My Dad, My Granddad, & Me

By Antoinette Lawrence & Terry Lewis

2016

To my brother, Arthur J. Wright, you are an awesome dad.
To Christian and Elijah, Aunt T.T. loves you.
Special thanks to M. Edwards and A. Norris for your extra set of eyes.
And to Lauren Lacy for your creativity.
A.L.

First and foremost, I'd like to thank the mighty Creator for making
this book possible.

To my deceased grandfathers who are constantly looking over
me in heaven, and to the entire "LEE" family.

A special thanks to my grandmothers Lydia Davis and Ruth Terry.
Mother-Brenda Broom (love you so much).
Sister-Tamico Lee-Spears (Love you big Nick).
Father-Louis Terry (Thanks for always listening to me no matter
the situation). Aunt-Mary Booker (God bless you for being so strong).
Thank you all for your love and support and for always
pushing me to reach my greatest potential.

I sincerely love all of you guys.
T.L.

My two favorite people in the whole wide world are my Dad, and my Granddad.

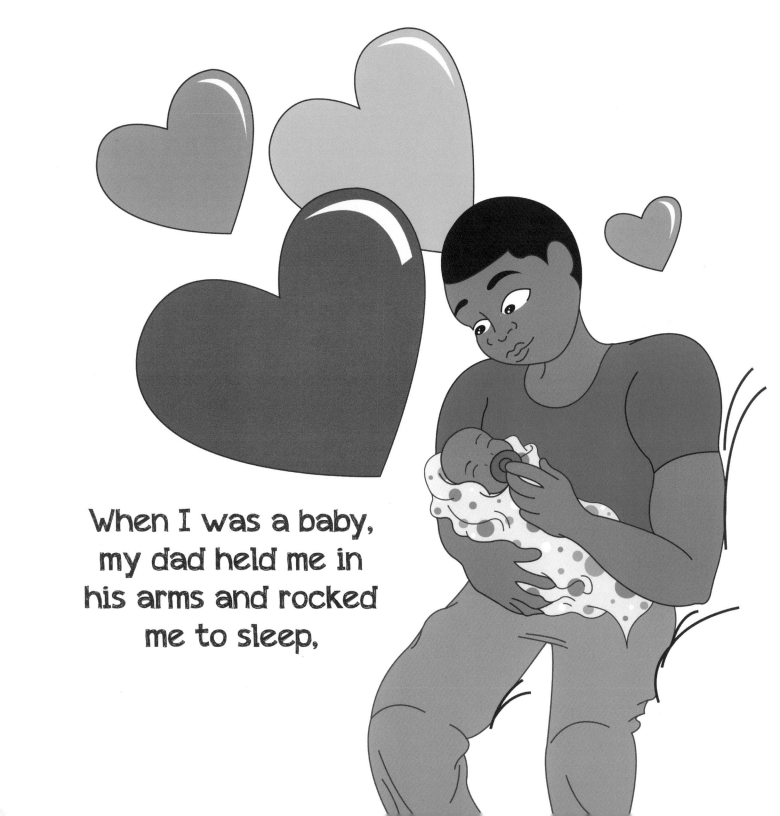

When I was a baby, my dad held me in his arms and rocked me to sleep,

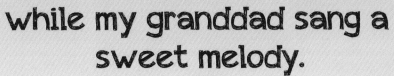

while my granddad sang a
sweet melody.

When I turned two, my dad and my granddad took me to the barbershop to get my first haircut.

My dad had to hold my arms,
while my granddad held my legs.

My granddad was a famous dancer when he was younger,

so he loved teaching my dad
and me how to dance.

On my first day of
kindergarten,
I was nervous and scared,

but my dad held my hand and walked me to my classroom.

I remember going to work with my dad for the first time.

By the middle of the day, he was calling my mom to pick me up.

I remember my granddad teaching
me how to tie my shoe,

and my dad showing me how
to tie a tie.

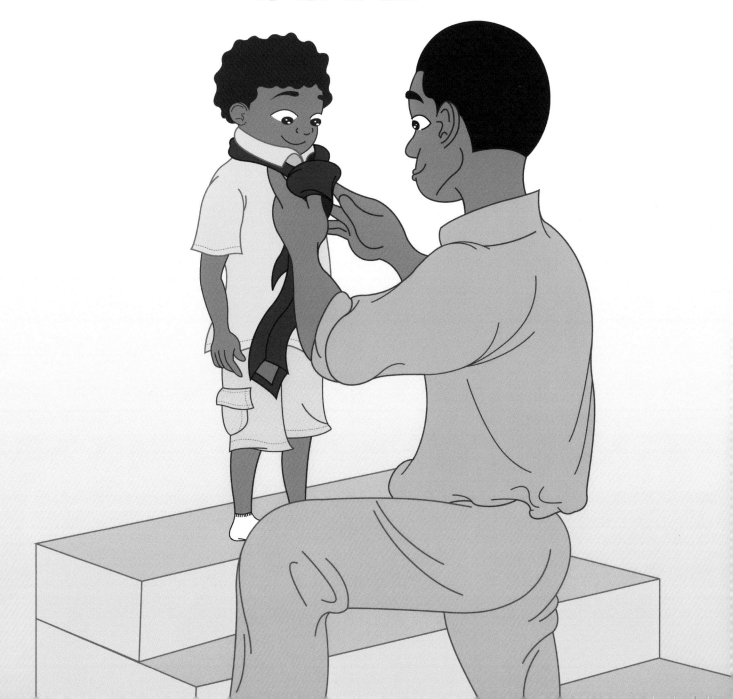

When I played my first football game, I remember hearing my dad and granddad screaming my name.

When I was little my
granddad taught me how
to ride a bike,

and my dad cheered me on.

When I was a little boy,
my granddad took me
on a fishing trip,

and showed me how to put the slimy worm on a hook to catch a fish.

When I was a little boy, my granddad loved telling me stories about his teenage years,

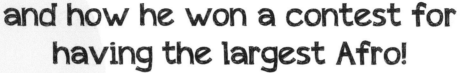

and how he won a contest for
having the largest Afro!

and riding on the roller coaster for the first time.

One summer, my family went on a camping trip, and the men were in charge of putting up the tent.

When the tent fell down, everyone
blamed it all on my dad, my granddad, and me.

The End

CPSIA information can be obtained at www.ICGtesting.com
Printed in the USA
BVIW12n0009200716
456167BV00004B/6